NO, NO, ROSINA

As far back as Rosina could remember, she wanted to go out on her father's fishing boat. "No, no, Rosina," said Papa. "A woman on a fishing boat brings bad luck." How Rosina manages to go to sea makes exciting reading, and when the last crab pot is raised there is a surprise for everyone.

The illustrations in this book are authentic San Francisco scenes. Here are some of them:

Page 2, Mile Rock Lighthouse, at the south end of the Golden Gate Bridge.

Page 3, The Farallon Islands, 30 to 40 miles off the San Francisco coast.

Pages 6 and 7, Looking east toward the Pacific Ocean; Fort Point on the left, Lime Point on the right, Point Bonita in the distance.

Page 12, Seal Rocks, San Francisco.

Pages 36 and 37, Heading west into San Francisco Bay under the Golden Gate Bridge, the San Francisco skyline in prospect.

Page 38, Alcatraz Island, San Francisco Bay.

NO, NO, ROSINA

by Patricia Miles Martin

illustrated by Earl Thollander

G.P. Putnam's Sons, New York

To Fran Seiden

Second Impression

Text © 1964 by Patricia Miles Martin
Illustrations © 1964 by Earl Thollander
Library of Congress Catalog Card Number: 64-12150
All rights reserved
MANUFACTURED IN THE UNITED STATES OF AMERICA
Published simultaneously in the Dominion of Canada
by Longmans Canada Limited, Toronto
07210

The time of day Rosina liked best was half-past three in the morning, for that was when the shouting started in her family.

"Up," said Mama. "Everybody up. Breakfast will be ready before you are dressed."

"Hit the deck," said Luigi.

"Rise and shine," said Carlo.

"Up," shouted Papa. "We have work to do."

"And may you have good luck, and a good catch today," said Mama.

5

As long as Rosina could remember, she had
wanted to go with her father and brothers on
their fishing boat, which sailed from
Fisherman's Wharf in San Francisco Bay.
Every winter from November to early
spring they went for crabs. Often she
heard them tell about it.

There, out in the sea beyond the Golden Gate, were their own crab traps — crab pots they were called, and orange-colored floats marked the water where they lay deep on the bottom of the ocean.

Every time she asked to go see for herself,
Papa said No.

"Why can't I?" she asked. "I could help."

And Papa always said, "No, no, Rosina. It is not a question of helping. I have enough help-ers. I have the Uncle. And when there is no school, I have Luigi and Carlo."

11

Rosina thought about Luigi and Carlo, lucky big brothers who went with their father on Saturdays and for the whole of winter vacation week, unless they had work to do on the wharf.

But she, Rosina, a fisherman's daughter who was named for the most beautiful fishing boat in the fleet, had never once been to sea.

Now, vacation week would soon be over and she would be back in school. So Rosina asked the same old question.

"Papa, can I go?"

Papa shouted, "You ask again?" He reached toward the ceiling. "The little one asks again."

"Your place is at home," Mama said.

"But when Luigi and Carlo are gone, I'm lonesome," Rosina said.

"Cheer up," said Carlo, "next week we'll all be back in school."

"But what about now?" Rosina asked.

"No, no, Rosina," said Luigi. "A fishing boat is no place for a girl."

"A woman on a fishing boat brings bad luck," Papa shouted.

"But she's such a small woman, maybe she wouldn't count," said Carlo.

While she ate her breakfast, Rosina thought about the talk of the morning. This time, when she asked to go, Papa had not said no. At least, not exactly.

When she had eaten, she slipped on her woolliest sweater and went outside to smell the fog. Lights in little windows along their street shone dimly. And down at the end of the street was Fisherman's Wharf, where the fishing fleet nodded sleepily in its lagoon.

Then Rosina knew what she must do.

She must show Papa that she wouldn't bring bad luck. Quickly, quietly, she would go aboard the *Santa Rosa*.

Papa and her brothers were still at the table. She listened a moment to be sure. Then she ran along the sidewalk straight for the wharf.

There, in the early morning fog, the *Santa Rosa* waited, nudging the ladder that led down

from the dock. Rosina swung down and stepped
aboard. She looked around for a place to hide.

On deck was the big, square, wooden crab box, ready for the day's catch. There, inside the cabin was an old coat on a hook — almost as though it were waiting for Rosina. She stepped behind it and its folds covered her.

The wharf was waking.

Fishermen were calling to each other.

"Where is Giusèppe?" one asked.

And Rosina heard Uncle's answer. "He has engine trouble. He can't go out today."

Then Papa and Uncle were aboard.

"Warm the motor," Papa shouted.

Rosina felt the shiver of the *Santa Rosa*.

Luigi and Carlo were coming down the ladder with packages of squid for bait.

"All ready," shouted Papa. He backed the *Santa Rosa* from her berth and they chugged from the lagoon into the Bay, on under the Golden Gate Bridge and into the ocean.

Finally Papa shouted, "Here's our trap line—"

The boat rocked in the water, and they were
bringing up the first crab pot.

"Lots of crabs," Luigi said.

This was the time for Rosina. "Guess who's
here," she said.

"We have a stowaway!" said Carlo.

"It's a little crab named Rosina," Luigi said.

Papa opened his mouth to shout, but no words
came. He lifted his hands to the sky. He held
his head. He was very angry.

Rosina spoke loudly to be heard above the noise of wind and sea. "I wanted to show you that I wouldn't bring bad luck."

Her father found his voice. "I will talk to you later about this." He turned to the Uncle. "Radio ashore and say to tell Mama that we have Rosina." He looked at Luigi and Carlo. "Why do we stand doing nothing?" he shouted. "We have work to do."

Luigi emptied the crabs into the wooden box.
"They look small," said Carlo.

"They *are* small," said Uncle. "Not one is big enough to keep."

"See what has happened," shouted Papa. "There should have been twenty or thirty big crabs maybe."

"Perhaps the next crab pot will be full of big ones," Carlo said.

Uncle threw the little crabs into the sea, and Luigi reached for squid to bait the empty pot. Uncle dropped the crab pot into the sea where it sank to the bottom, below its marker.

They chugged on to the second float.

Luigi and Carlo, handsome in slickers and hats and high rubber boots, brought up the second crab pot.

On the ocean were their own orange-colored floats — so many — Rosina thought — more than a hundred — Papa had said so —

Through the mist were other fishing boats, dozens and dozens of boats, all working with their own crab traps.

Sea gulls flew low overhead and a green frothy wave struck the side of the boat. Rosina tasted salt spray. Over San Francisco the sky grew pink.

She wondered what they would find in the second crab pot. Perhaps Papa would forget to be angry if they had a good catch.

When the crab pot was pulled aboard, Rosina saw a few small crabs inside the wire cage.

Papa groaned loudly.

"Look at them," he said. "Not one is big
enough to keep."

Carlo tossed the little crabs back into the ocean. "I see a bottle riding a wave," he said. "It's a corked bottle and it's coming this way."

Luigi grabbed a hand net and waited until he could scoop it from the sea. "There's a paper inside." He pulled a small roll of paper from the narrow neck of the bottle.

" 'I'm a fisherman's son,' " he read. " 'I live in Monterey.' The boy gives his name and his age. He says, 'Will you write to me?' And he signs it, 'Your friend.' "

"Out of the sea, we find a pen pal," said Papa. "So. We return home with a catch of one friend."

Papa was still angry. "Nothing but foolishness today," he said.

The boat churned on through the sea to the third marker.

Luigi and Carlo brought up the crab pot.

"These look better," said Uncle.

Quickly, he and Papa sorted them. "Twenty-three large crabs," Papa shouted.

It was the same with the fourth trap, and the fifth. All morning they worked. The big crabs went into the square wooden crab box, and the little ones were tossed into the sea. Each time, the crab pot was baited with squid and lowered over the side, where it sank deep in the water beneath its float.

"Tomorrow, our crab pots will be full again," Rosina said. "We have had good luck today."

Papa didn't answer.

Carlo spoke softly. "Look at the crabs, Papa. For whatever the reason, we have a good catch. She brought no bad luck."

When the last crab pot was raised,
it was filled with fine big crabs.

"And we've got
another stowaway,"
said Carlo.

"AN OCTOPUS," said Rosina. "An octopus for supper." She looked at Papa. "Today, you caught hundreds and hundreds of crabs. And an octopus. And you found a letter in a bottle." She thought of the boy in Monterey. "How old is the boy who wrote the letter?"

"He's thirteen," said Luigi.

"Then Carlo will send the answer," Rosina said.

Papa spoke. "Already, Rosina gives the orders. I, I only, give orders here." He pointed a finger at Carlo. "Yes, you will write to the boy. Wish him good luck and good fishing."

When the fog cleared entirely and the sun was high in a blue sky, they headed for the wharf. The wooden crab box was full.

Rosina knew that she could never again ask Papa to go on the *Santa Rosa.* This was a day she would always remember. She would enjoy it to the last minute. She waved at other fishing boats. She waved at a party boat as it passed.

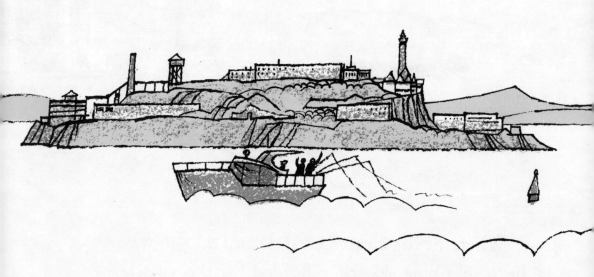

SANTA ROSA

When they reached home, Papa talked with her.

At the end of his talk, he said, "And now you will speak with Mama."

"I'm sorry," Rosina said to Mama. "I'll never go anywhere, not even with Papa and Luigi and Carlo, without telling you first."

"Good," said Mama. "Now we will forget that you have done this."

Rosina didn't really forget. She was dreaming of crabs and the salt smell of the sea when the alarm clock rang the next morning.

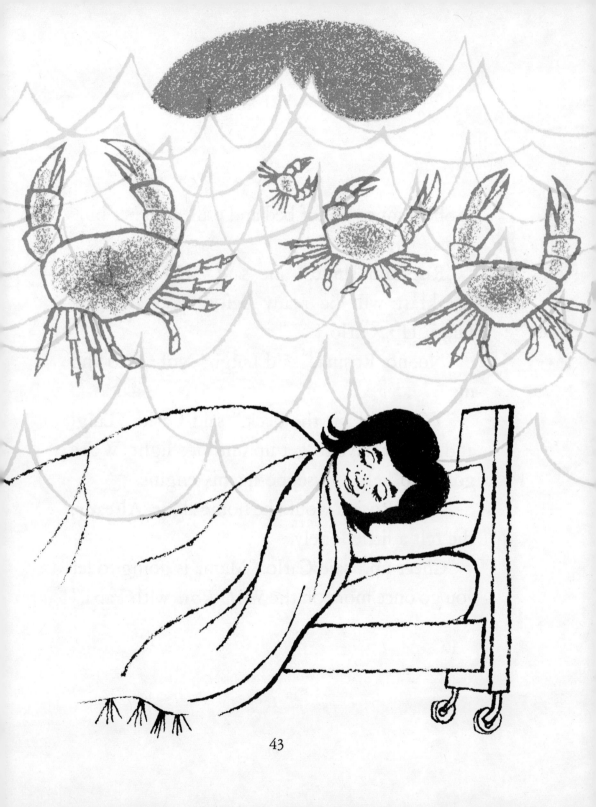

She jumped out of bed and pulled on her blue jeans.

"Rise and shine," she said. "Hit the deck. Breakfast will be ready before you are. Up, Luigi. Up, Carlo."

"No, no, Rosina," said Luigi. "Not Carlo and me."

"YOU will hit the deck," said Carlo. "Luigi and I don't have to get up until it's light. We're going to help Giusèppe fix his engine."

Again, Rosina would be home alone. Already, she felt a little lonely.

"Cheer up," said Carlo. "Mama is going to let you go once more on the *Santa Rosa* with Papa."

Rosina was too happy to talk.

She put on Luigi's slicker. She wore Carlo's hat.

Papa was shouting.

"Fix a good lunch, Mama," he said, as he patted the top of Carlo's hat.

"Fix a good lunch for
me and my crew."

The Author

PATRICIA MILES MARTIN and her husband live in San Mateo, California, where she writes six days a week in a pantry-turned-office. She describes herself as a "compulsive writer," having had her first poem accepted by the newspaper in Monette, Missouri, when she was seven years old. Now she reviews children's books in several well-known newspapers throughout the United States.

Mrs. Martin wrote poetry until 1957, and then started writing children's fiction. She has been most successful and has had more than a dozen books published for young people. Her most recent books include *Abraham Lincoln, Pocahontas, The Lucky Little Porcupine, Show and Tell, The Raccoon and Mrs. McGinnis,* and *Benjie Goes into Business.*

The Artist

EARL THOLLANDER was born in Kingsburg, California, and educated in San Francisco. He began serious training as an artist at the City College of San Francisco and subsequently attended various colleges for art training. After spending two years in the Navy aboard a landing ship where he managed to sketch and paint, he learned basic advertising art techniques before taking a position as an artist with the San Francisco *Examiner.* Mr. Thollander is an avid traveler and he especially enjoys working "on location." For this book he spent a day sailing out to sea in a crab fishing boat. Mr. Thollander lives with his wife and two children in a house which overlooks San Francisco Bay.